T 7950   17091

DATE DUE

JUL 2 3 1997			
SEP – 6 1997			
AUG. 1 1 2004			
SEP. 2 8 2005			
JUL 0 2 2007			
DEC 3 1 2012			
JUN 1 1 2015			
NOV 3 0 2015			

F
McM   McMorrow, Catherine
        Gold fever!

A NOTE TO PARENTS

When your children are ready to "step into reading," giving them the right books is as crucial as giving them the right food to eat. **Step into Reading Books** present exciting stories and information reinforced with lively, colorful illustrations that make learning to read fun, satisfying, and worthwhile. They are priced so that acquiring an entire library of them is affordable. And they are beginning readers with a difference— they're written on five levels.

Early Step into Reading Books are designed for brand-new readers, with large type and only one or two lines of very simple text per page. **Step 1 Books** feature the same easy-to-read type as the Early Step into Reading Books, but with more words per page. **Step 2 Books** are both longer and slightly more difficult, while **Step 3 Books** introduce readers to paragraphs and fully developed plot lines. **Step 4 Books** offer exciting nonfiction for the increasingly independent reader.

The grade levels assigned to the five steps—preschool through kindergarten for the Early Books, preschool through grade 1 for Step 1, grades 1 through 3 for Step 2, grades 2 through 3 for Step 3, and grades 2 through 4 for Step 4—are intended only as guides. Some children move through all five steps very rapidly; others climb the steps over a period of several years. Either way, these books will help your child "step into reading" in style!

Text copyright © 1996 by Catherine McMorrow. Illustrations copyright © 1996 by Michael Eagle. All rights reserved under International and Pan-American Copyright Conventions. Published in the United States by Random House, Inc., New York, and simultaneously in Canada by Random House of Canada Limited, Toronto.
Library of Congress Cataloging-in-Publication Data
McMorrow, Catherine.
Gold fever! / by Catherine McMorrow ; illustrated by Michael Eagle.
p. cm—(Step into reading. Step 4 book)
ISBN 0-679-86432-6 (trade)—ISBN 0-679-96432-0 (lib. bdg.)
[1. California—Gold discoveries—Juvenile literature.]
I. Title. II. Series. III. Series: Eagle, Michael, ill.
F865.M39 1996
979.4'04—dc20 93-34694

Printed in the United States of America 10 9 8 7 6 5 4 3 2 1

STEP INTO READING is a trademark of Random House, Inc.

17091

Step into Reading

GOLD FEVER!

A Step 4 Book

by Catherine McMorrow
illustrated by Michael Eagle

Random House 🏠 New York

Chapter 1
Gold!

It was a cold morning in California. James Marshall stared down into a rushing stream. The water ran from the American River to a new sawmill. Marshall was the carpenter who had built the mill. He had often told his workers, "There are minerals here. Maybe silver, maybe gold." But the men just laughed at him.

Suddenly, he saw something sparkle! He knelt down. There! A yellow gleam on the bottom! And another! Marshall's heart pounded. Flecks of gold were shining on the rocks and in the cracks between them.

Marshall scooped up a nugget and galloped downriver. He would show them to John Sutter, the owner of the sawmill. He burst into Sutter's office.

"We must lock ourselves in a private room!" he cried.

Sutter thought, "This fellow has gone loony!" But he bolted the door. He even pushed a dresser against it!

Sutter peered at the nugget.

"Well," he said, "it *looks* like gold. Let's test it."

He got down an encyclopedia.

He read that gold is softer than any other metal. A piece of gold the size of a pea can be stretched into a wire that is two miles long. Gold can be pounded so thin that you can see a greenish light shining through it. Gold is eight times heavier than stones and sand. Gold is sturdy, yet soft. It will not rust or tarnish.

Sutter and Marshall tested the rock. They pounded it. It flattened easily—just like gold. They weighed it. It was heavier than a whole handful of silver coins. They rubbed acid on it to see if it would rust or tarnish. Nothing happened!

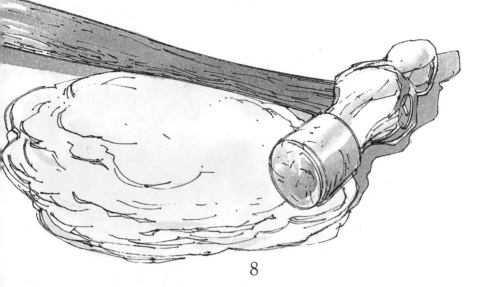

Marshall got wild with excitement. He spun around the room. "Gold! Gold!" But John Sutter was grim. He had vineyards and fields and cattle. He knew that his workers would run off to hunt for gold. Gold would change everything.

"Please!" he begged Marshall. "Keep this a secret for six weeks!" At least the spring planting would get done.

But who could keep such an exciting secret?

Sutter himself was bursting with it. He strutted around, bragging. He wrote to a Spanish friend, "Something important has happened!"

Marshall couldn't keep the secret, either. He told his workers, "By God, boys, it is the pure stuff!" The workers told everyone who visited them. The visitors talked about it everywhere they went.

Gold fever broke out in the West!

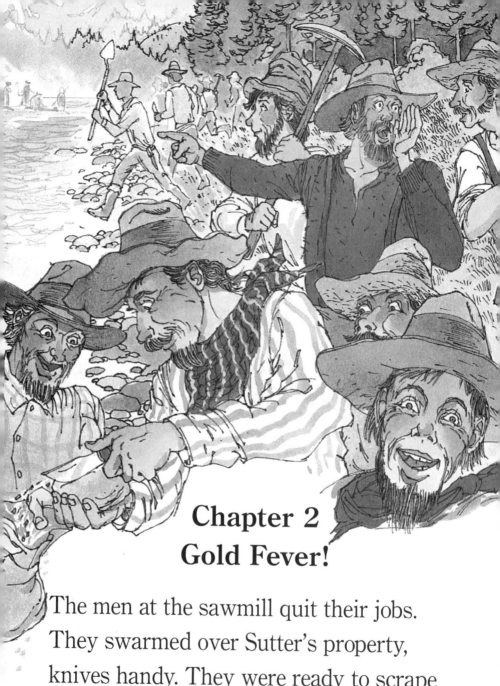

Chapter 2
Gold Fever!

The men at the sawmill quit their jobs.
They swarmed over Sutter's property,
knives handy. They were ready to scrape
gold flakes into their leather pouches.

John Sutter wandered sadly about.

Tools lay on the ground. Houses stood half-finished. Fields lay half-planted.

"They all left me," Sutter wrote in his diary. "Everyone from the clerk to the cook."

Some Mormons who had worked for Sutter went downriver. They found a lot of gold in a sandbar. In one week, they took out gold worth $49,000. Today, this much gold would be worth more than half a million dollars!

One Mormon named Sam Brannan took a bottle of gold dust to San Francisco.

"Gold! Gold!" he shouted, walking up and down the streets. "Gold in the American River!"

At that time, there were only 900 people living in San Francisco. And they all caught gold fever! Doctors, lawyers, tailors, blacksmiths, and wheelbarrow-makers all became miners. They headed for the gold fields around Sutter's sawmill and the rivers of central California.

The famous frontier scout Kit Carson carried an official report all the way to Washington, D.C.

On December 5, 1848, President James Polk announced to the nation: "It's true! Amazing riches have been discovered in California!"

The East exploded with Gold Fever! In Boston, New York City, and Philadelphia, the rumors flew.

"You can pull a bush out of the earth— and gold nuggets are stuck to the roots!"

"The people are running all over the country, picking gold out of the earth like a thousand hogs rooting up nuts."

"Eastern streams have fish, but California's streams are full of gold!"

Merchants sold special money belts for gold, "California saddles," and Indian Vegetable Pills to cure sickness on the trail.

Newspapers advertised: "Hooray for California! Get our California Gold Grease! Only $10 a box! Rub on your body, roll down a hill. Gold, *and gold only,* will stick to your skin!"

Factories made pickaxes, shovels, boots, and biscuits. One miner even bought a diving suit—so he could stroll along the river bottom, picking up nuggets!

"Gold! Gold! Gold!" The wild cry echoed throughout the East. Men left their wives and children, jobs, cows, and fields. They formed a human tidal wave going west.

"Don't worry!" they told their families. "We'll be back with our pockets full of gold!"

Chapter 3
The Gold Rush: By Land

For most gold-seekers, California was 3,000 miles away. Today, you can fly that distance in about six hours. Back then, it took weeks.

In 1849, there were only thirty states in the Union. Between the Missouri River and California, there was nothing but wilderness.

The "Forty-niners," as newspapers called them, hitched oxen or mules to their wagons. They saddled up their horses, laced up their walking boots, and faced the prairie. They started out singing.

But the dust on the trail became twelve inches deep. It got in their eyes, up their noses, and down their pants. They got headaches, leg aches, backaches, and sore feet. No one felt like singing anymore.

The Forty-niners ate moldy beans and bacon for breakfast, lunch, and dinner. Sometimes they got a treat—buffalo pot pie, or bush fish, otherwise known as rattlesnake!

Tired and crabby, the men fought with each other. Sometimes they fought hostile Indians. But many men were not skilled at frontier life. They shot themselves just picking up a rifle. Men fell sick with cholera and died. They had to cross swollen rivers. The rapid currents pulled men and animals under. Many drowned.

The Forty-niners pushed on through
prairie fires, lightning, and thunderstorms.
They trudged through seas of mud and
storms of hail as big as golf balls.

After the prairie came the burning
desert. Day after day, the men dragged
onward without water. The blazing sun
dried their skin till it cracked. Their

tongues swelled. Graves, dead animals, and abandoned supplies marked the trail.

Sometimes they saw beautiful green trees and blue water in the distance. But it was only a mirage. Once the oxen were so thirsty that they ran toward it. After a few minutes, the mirage faded and the oxen fell dead.

At last the Forty-niners came out of the desert. The grass and cool streams of the foothills lifted their spirits. But not for long! The "High Sierras"—and winter— loomed ahead. Wagons had to be unloaded and dragged up steep slopes, then let down over rocky ledges by ropes.

Ice coated everything. Snow fell and blew in deep drifts, hiding all firewood. There were no animals to shoot for food. The men ate boiled deer hooves and little birds. They burned wagon parts to keep warm. Through it all, they continued to dream of one thing only: California gold!

Chapter 4
The Gold Rush: By Sea

Others came by water. They sailed down around South America and up the western coast, a long, hard voyage.

Men piled on board clipper ships, rebuilt whalers, and half-rotted barks. If it would float, they sailed it!

Belowdecks it was smelly and hard to breathe. Only the rats liked it. The men came up on deck for fresh air. But on deck, the wind slapped them with icy water.

The trip could take six long months. The food got wormy, the water slimy. Many fell sick with scurvy and cholera. The dead were buried at sea.

There was a shortcut across the
Isthmus of Panama, the little strip of land
that connects North and South America.
Men got off their ships on the eastern side
and hiked to the western side. There they
waited to catch another ship up to California.

But the Isthmus was sixty miles of thick jungle. It was steaming hot, swarming with mosquitoes, fleas, snakes, wildcats, crocodiles, spiders, and thieves.

Many Forty-niners got tropical fever. But gold fever pushed them onward!

Not only Americans caught gold fever. Men came from Europe, China, Russia, and Australia. But no matter where they came from, they all began to look alike.

Forty-niners grew beards. They wore red flannel shirts, wide-brimmed hats, and high boots. They carried pistols, pickaxes, and bowie knives. By the time they got to California, they were exhausted and penniless. But they came to get rich.

Chapter 5
The Gold Fields

At first, there was room for everyone. A miner could pick any spot. He marked the corners of his claim with stakes topped by tin cans or rags.

There were no laws or police, just a few simple rules. If you stole, you got thirty-nine lashes or your ears were cut off—unless you were hanged!

Getting gold out of the earth wasn't easy. It had to be "washed." The simplest method was panning. A miner scooped gravel and water into a shallow pan or bowl. Quickly but gently, he moved the pan in circles to swirl the dirt out with the water. The heavy gold stayed in the bottom. Panning took hours. Only a small amount of dirt could be washed at one time.

Miners also washed gold in a cradle, a wooden box with screens on top and ridges on the bottom. They shoveled in dirt and poured water over it, then rocked the cradle back and forth. Stones got caught in the screen. The lighter gravel fell through and was washed away by the water. The heavy gold got caught on the ridges.

There were also "Long Toms." A Long Tom was a great big cradle. It took more than one man to work the Long Tom.

In the beginning, lots of miners found gold.

One fellow dug a hole four feet deep. He sat in it all day, digging with a spoon. He piled nugget after nugget into a wooden bowl. He got so tired of digging, he let someone else take a turn!

Another man dug a trench and hit a ground squirrel nest. Instead of nuts, the squirrel had stored golden nuggets!

A ten-year-old boy named Perkins picked up a stone for his slingshot. It was a chunk of gold worth one thousand dollars.

A man called Hance chased his mule down a hill. He tripped on a gold rock. It weighed fourteen pounds. Another rock found on that same hill weighed 195 pounds! It was the largest nugget ever found in America. Today it would be worth $1,229,592!

Most of the miners were in a hurry to collect their fortunes and head home.

A few took time to build cabins. The rest slept in tents, lean-tos, or holes in the ground.

They ate dried beef softened in water. Who had time to hunt game or plant vegetables? There was gold to dig!

Merchants came. They traded dried
peaches, pickles, and onions for the
miners' gold. Their prices were sky-high.
A single egg might cost three dollars!

Gamblers and cardsharps came too.
They put up tent saloons and hired
musicians. The miners were glad to hear
music! They paid a pinch of gold dust for
whiskey and played cards all night. Much
of the gold that the miners took out of the
ground ended up in the gamblers' pockets!

By 1850, 100,000 people had come to
California. The gold fields were crowded.
The "easy pickin's" were gone.

Men worked long hours shoveling dirt
and hauling water. Fingers and toes got
smashed by rocks. Men stood knee-deep in

icy water. Their legs froze. The fiery sun scorched their backs. Forty-niners worked harder but found less gold. They grew discouraged. Many men looked for other work.

One ex-miner knew how lonely people got when they were so far from home. He started an "express mail" service. He made a list of miners' names. Then he rode his pony to the San Francisco post office. There he collected the mail and brought it back to camp. It took six days. He charged fifty cents a letter.

One woman found a cracked old washboard. She made $900 in a week doing people's laundry!

Another lady made $18,000 selling meat and fruit pies.

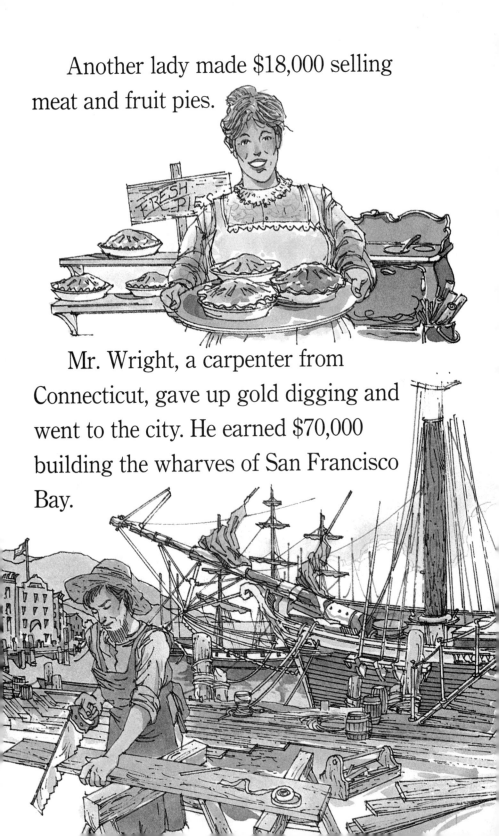

Mr. Wright, a carpenter from Connecticut, gave up gold digging and went to the city. He earned $70,000 building the wharves of San Francisco Bay.

When gold was first discovered, San Francisco was a sleepy village. Two years later, 25,000 people lived and worked there.

The harbor was crammed with abandoned ships. The sailors, and even the captains, had run off to the gold fields.

Some of the deserted ships were hauled to shore and used as buildings. Doors and windows were cut out to make a bank, a church, and a city jail.

Before the Gold Rush, people thought California was a wasteland full of grizzly bears.

After the Gold Rush, it became one of the richest and most populated areas on the continent.

In 1850, California became a state, with an established government and laws.

And what happened to John Sutter? Squatters took his land. Strangers stole his cattle. He did not do well as a gold miner. He had many debts. In 1857, he moved east to Pennsylvania.

James Marshall, who found the first gold, wandered from place to place, hunting for more. He didn't have much luck, either. Building and fixing things was what Marshall did best. But history will always remember him as "The Discoverer," the man who started gold fever raging.

The great California Gold Rush lasted
from 1848 to 1859. A total of $81 million in
gold was taken from the streams and hills
of central California.

By the 1860s, the mines were empty.
Women and children came. Homes and
churches were built. Men were busy
running new businesses.

Then one day, someone found a lot of "blue stuff" in the Comstock lode in Nevada. "Silver!" the cry went up. "Silver!"